C000083838

R.O.V.

REVIVAL OF VENUS

ERIC WILKINS

Copyright © 2021 Eric Wilkins

ISBN:
978-1-952874-57-4 (paperback)
978-1-952874-58-1 (hardback)
978-1-952874-59-8 (ebook)

All rights reserved. No part of this publication may be reproduced,
stored in a retrieval system, or transmitted in any form or by any
means - electronic, mechanical, photocopy, recording, scanning,
or other – except for brief quotations in critical reviews or articles,
without the prior written permission of the publisher.

Published by:

OMNIBOOK CO.
99 Wall Street, Suite 118
New York, NY 10005
USA
+1-866-216-9965
www.omnibookcompany.com

For e-book purchase: Kindle on Amazon, Barnes and Noble
Book purchase: Amazon.com, Barnes & Noble, and
www.omnibookcompany.com

Omnibook titles may be purchased in bulk for educational, business,
fund-raising, or sales promotional use. For more information please
e-mail info@omnibookcompany.com

CONTENTS

CHAPTER 1

The Antimatter Repulse Attracter Emitter Invention

It had all been speculated by many astronomers and the passage of time, that the planet Venus seemed different than all the other planets in the solar system.

No scientific mind of Earth's twenty seven earlier centuries had ever figured out exactly what happened in the past to make Venus the hottest slowly retrograde rotating planet in our own solar system.

There came a time in the twenty eighth century, when a long termed project had begun to attempt to repair and reevaluate the mysterious world of Planet Venus.

Citizens of Earth had progressed greatly in space exploration to the point of several Mars bases and orbiting space stations around Ganymede and Europa but Venus and it's thick crushing atmosphere had forever been a forbidden planet for humans to land on and survive.

In the year 2817, hundreds of space flights leaving and entering Earth's atmosphere were a normal occurrence. There were at least a hundred orbital stations around Earth at different altitudes including two paraplegic hospital stations in low Earth orbit.

Ganymede and Europa, both had research stations around two of Jupiter's Moons. The Mars colonies had excelled and expanded until several thousand Mars families now lived and prospered in three pressurized domed cities on Planet Mars.

Humans of all nations had stopped their long time warring ways and joined together to colonize and conquer space in the immediate solar system.

No one had conquered Venus because to this present date's technology, it had not been possible for humans to survive the hostel hellish Venus crushing poisonous atmosphere.

In the year 2820, a young Einstein of the day scientist named Christina Barbarosa, had discovered how to use a tiny amount of antimatter to form a huge reverse pulsed beam that was very powerful even in the vacuum of space. She named it the ARAE for Antimatter Repulse Attracter Emitter.

It is to that brilliant discovery, that is what lead up to the Earth Astronomy Space Council that convened on this present Earth day of March 7 2821.

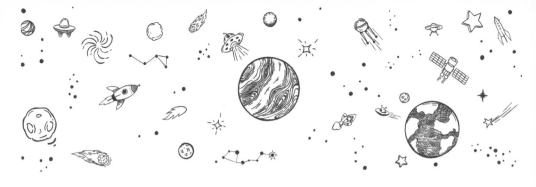

CHAPTER 2
Professor Dario Omagus Speaks about Venus

Professor Dario Omagus gaveled the large body of scientific minds to a complete silence as he began this session of the greatest scientific importance to all humankind.

Today, we scientist are gathered here to create plans for the future Revival of Venus Project he stated.

In all of my years of studying astronomy, I and many others have always wondered about the mysteries of Planet Venus and why it exist in the drastic state that it does.

The cyber world and the scientific body in attendance listened intently.

Here are some facts about Venus that are presently known. He continued.

The planet Venus from Earth has an apparent magnitude of -3.8 to -4.6, which makes it visible from Earth even on a clear day.

Venus is sometimes referred to as the morning star and the evening star. This all dates back to ancient civilizations who believed that Venus was in fact two different stars appearing in the sky.

Once the orbit of Venus overtakes Earth's orbit, it changes from being visible at sunrise to being visible at sunset. To the ancients of Earth, they were known as Phosphorus and Hesperus by Greek astronomers and the Romans referred to them as Lucifer and Vesper

At present, a single day on Venus is longer than its own yearly revolve. That's because due to the slow retrograde rotation of Venus on its axis, it takes 243 Earth-days to complete one retrograde rotation while Venus' orbit of the Sun only takes 225 Earth-days making a year on Venus shorter than a day on Venus.

Venus is sometimes called Earth's sister planet. This is because their sizes are very similar. There is only a 638 km or 396.4 miles smaller difference in the diameter of Venus than the diameter of Earth and Venus has around 81% of Earth's mass.

The two planets are also similarly located in the solar system with Venus being the closest planet to Earth than any other planet. Both planets also have a central iron core and a molten mantle and similar crust.

Planet Venus has no moons. That's a problem Professor Omagus stated.

Billions of years ago, the climate of Venus may have been similar to that of Earth and scientists believe that Venus once possessed large amounts of water or oceans. However, due to the high temperatures produced from the extreme greenhouse effect, this water boiled off long ago and the surface of the planet is now too hot and hostile to sustain life as we know it.

Venus rotates slowly in the opposite direction to other planets in the solar system. Most planets rotate counter-clockwise on their axis looking down from their north poles however, Venus like Uranus, rotates clockwise.

This is known as a retrograde rotation and according to ancient science theory, may have been caused by a collision with an asteroid or other object which crashed into Venus and caused the planet to change its rotational rate and direction of spin. Possible it may have even caused Venus to flip upside down.

Professor Omagus paused in his lengthily Venus fact explanation and injected a personal opinion to the many scientist that listening intently.

You know what he paused. I find it hard to comprehend why astronomers from the twenty first century, always tried to explain all the solar system's properties by postulating a collision with another heavenly body.

Indeed, that may be true in some cases he conjectured but, close passes without collisions could very well have changed planet properties also and I professor Omagus surmise that this may have been what happened long ago to cause the present status of Venus.

Personally, I think that Venus stopped rotating eastward when it lost it's moon that we now refer to as Planet Mercury. Possible if Mercury was once Venus' Moon, maybe another massive object passed near without colliding and caused the then Mercury moon to be pulled into its own inner orbit around the Sun. After all, Mercury does indeed have a very unique mysterious elliptical orbit.

A heavenly body massive enough to pass on the outside of Venus' then Moon, lets say estimated at approximately a half million miles above Venus, would surly cause the Venus poles to reverse when the former Mercury Moon was pulled away by the gravity well of a close passing massive body.

Professor Omagus continued his facts lecture after stating his personal opinion. I have another postulation Professor Omagus stated.

Venus passes closer to Earth than any other planet. It's been theorized for years that Venus and Earth's close approach and gravity are too far away to perturb each other when they are at opposition. I think that there is something wrong with this theory.

It's not just two similar masses that are acting upon each other at close approach. The Earth has a Moon in orbit that also adds to the mass of the Earth system's gravity well.

Since Venus is 81% Earth's mass. The Earth's Moons mass has to be added to the equation also.

Possible, it's the Earth Moon total system mass that gives Venus a tug when Venus passes on the inside of Earth and the Moon's orbit and keeps Venus from being totally tidally locked to the Sun.

It's a well known fact that when Venus passes on the inside of Earth's orbit, that Venus always presents the same face or side towards our planet Earth. That indeed has to be a gravitational influence.

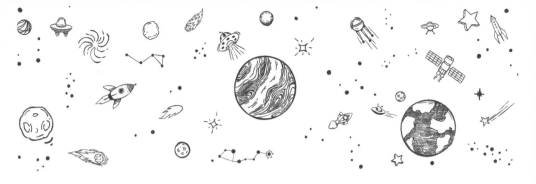

CHAPTER 3
More Venus Facts

Venus is the hottest planet in the solar system with an average surface temperature of 462°C (863°F). Also, Venus doesn't tilt on its axis which means there are no seasons either.

The atmosphere composition consist of a dense 96.5% carbon dioxide which traps heat and caused the greenhouse effect which evaporated any water sources billions of years ago.

It's the Earth's Moon that causes axial tilt and the season on our wonderful planet. Humankind wouldn't be able to exist for long if the Earth lost its Moon.

Venus is named after the Roman goddess of love and beauty. This may be in part due the brightness of the planet and may date back to the Babylonians in the year 1581 who referred to Venus as the bright queen of the sky.

The professor concluded his known Venus facts to his captivated audience and stated the following.

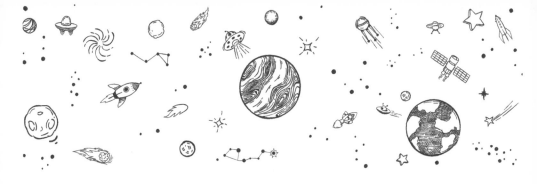

CHAPTER 4
Christina Barbarosa
The ARAE Inventor

We are here today to honor our esteemed scientist Christina Barbarosa, who's research that lead to the invention of the ARAE that can eject a reverse pulse or attractive force in a powerful focused beam towards any object.

It's predicted that future days will bring the powerful ARAE up to immeasurable repulsive and attractive strength.

I now present to you, Miss Christina Barbarosa. Lets give this respected scientist and her research team a round of applause for the discovery of a lifetime of the ARAE or Antimatter Repulse Attracter Emitter.

The attending crowd stood and gave her a standing ovation.

Tell us about your discovery Christina, Professor Omagus was still applauding as she stepped forward to address this world-wide broadcast announcement event.

CHAPTER 5
Antimatter Repulse Attracter Emitter

Hello my fellow colleagues. I Christina Barbarosa, am pleased today to be here with all of you to introduce this exciting new ARAE concept.

I and my dedicated staff, have devised a new repulse and attract device that has very unique properties that works extremely well even in the vacuum of space.

It was this amazing antimatter and string theory research discovery, that myself and other scientist here created in our long dedicated effort that took place over the past decade.

This antimatter discovery has enabled my staff as a team, to create the ARAE that myself and staff refer to simply as R A. or repulse attractor.

Well she stated, I'll attempt to express ARAE's power for all including the millions of cyber listeners that are tuned in today.

At full power and mounted on a space ship tug, it can push Earth sized planets around in their orbits and move moons to specific locations. How does it work she stated.

Let me explain. Our research team discovered that it only takes one negative antimatter liquid hydrogen atom to be bombarded with a positive charged helium three atom, to effect a three second reverse pulse that is capable of exerting a controllable focused bandwidth of extreme pressure or attraction outward or inward even in the vacuum of space.

You can call space a vacuum all you like she stated but, the fabric of space is not a nothing.

Space is indeed a fabric that bends in the presence of a planet or moon's massive body. Space is more like an Aether of tiny invisible to the eye inferred stringed particles of innumerable element strings. Space is never a nothing no matter where you are in the universe.

The fabric of space itself is indeed a powerful something when acted upon by the ARAE device.

Therefore, it can also be used as new space ship engines producing one quarter light speed of 46,500 miles per second with perpetual fueled use.

What's amazing Christina continued, is that the kick back ratio of the emitted pulse in a forward direction, is relatively nothing or less than one hundred of a percent compared to the forward pressure emitted force.

Interestingly, at the same time, if ejected at the rear of a ship, it enables a extremely powerful propulsion.

The ARAE system also has the capability of focusing in on specific atoms and pushing or attracting individual elements and atoms with out disturbing other atoms.

So, if you have ships that can produce repulsion at its nose or forward direction and propulsion at its rear without cancel, you then have a new ship capability of gradually moving large objects around in space and placing them wherever you want them to be.

Sure, it could be used as a weapon but that is not our intention here on the project that we are all here today to begin discussions about.

That project that we are here to begin is called,

The Revival of Venus or ROV. I now graciously give you back to Professor Omagus to explain the exact details. A standing ovation occurred again as Christina sat down and the professor stepped forward to speak again.

CHAPTER 6
ROV or Revival of Venus Plan

A silence came over the audience as Professor Omagus paused before speaking.

We of this century begin today this adventurous project entitled, Revival of Venus.

There are now in production, several fleets of ARAE powered ships that will soon begin the biggest ever undertaken by humanity project ever.

This important project to Revive the Planet Venus and make it habitable for future humankind is an undertaking that the ARAE discovery will allow us to undertake and begin immediately.

In the immediate future, fleets of R-A powered ships will be dispatched to Venus to focus their repulse attracter beams towards the upper atmosphere of the thick Venus atmosphere in order to begin the thinning process of the greenhouse atmosphere that is approximately 300 miles thick.

It's been postulated by several esteemed scientist, that by focusing the R-A beam towards specific atoms in the Venusians atmosphere, that in a half century or so of time, it will be possible to reduce the greenhouse effect and extreme pressure by blasting the unwanted gasses away from Venus and inward towards the Sun.

It's also predicted that this atmosphere regeneration will take approximately 50 earth years to complete.

The long term plan is to reduce the atmosphere of Venus by 66% over the half century process.

After the atmosphere is beginning to be thinned to specifications and Venus begins to cool, Repulse Attracter ships will begin the process of mining ice asteroids and injecting them into the Venus polar atmosphere to introduce water vapor back on the Venus surface for the first time in eons.

Also, during that long term process, Nitrogen and Oxygen will be continuously injected into the Venus' atmosphere. Because Venus hardly has any magnetosphere at the moment, it is intended to bring the millibars pressure down to just 10 % above earth's approximate thousand millibars pressure at the surface of Venus.

It is in later plans to remedy Venus' weak magnetosphere situation by inserting a similar sized earth moon into orbit which my head assistant Jack Wiseman will inform you of those future processes in the second phase of ROV. Mr. Jack Wiseman, it's all yours Sir, you have the floor.

More applause as the two scientist exchanged places.

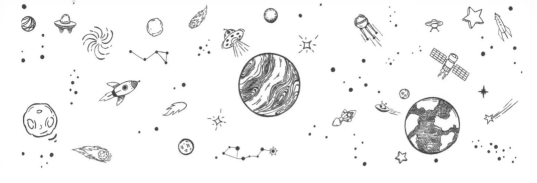

CHAPTER 7
Jack Wiseman
Phase Two of Revival of Venus

Hello all Mr. Wiseman said as he stepped forward to begin explaining phase two of the ROV project.

Jack Wiseman had been Christina's head consultant during the ten year antimatter research project.

His lecture began.

It is estimated that phase one will be accomplished in approximately fifteen years.

When Venus' atmosphere is reduced to our start specifications, the second phase of ROV will begin.

Venus needs a moon. We've all had long debates on which moon in our solar system would be best suited for Venus once it's atmosphere has began to be reduced.

We've considered Mercury in our intensive research but it has come to be known that there is a better alternative for Planet Venus than Mercury as a Venus moon.

That Moon would be Triton. Yes it would take longer to move Triton away from Neptune but Triton is the perfect size and has much nitrogen to be harvested for the atmosphere of Venus.

Triton's diameter is approximately 1632 miles and would be put in orbit above Venus at about 220,000 miles around Venus.

In a 26 day orbit around Venus, Triton would cause a 21 degree tilt of Venus' axis and cause Venus to have seasons.

Also, as Triton is carefully manipulated to within a half million miles of Venus, It will cause Planet Venus to reverse it's magnetic poles opposite that of Triton and begin rotating slowly counter clockwise from its north pole like the majority of the planets in our solar system.

In the year, 2845, humanity will be at the point of starting the process of removing Triton from Neptune and gracefully beginning the next important phase of the 15 year journey of transporting the retrograde moon Triton to a specific 26 day Venus orbit around Venus of approximately 2464 miles per hour in a eastward direction.

It is well known that as Triton gets closer to the inner solar system, much of its nitrogen will vaporized and leave a trail of much needed nitrogen to be captured and inserted into the Venus atmosphere by cargo vessels.

It is intended along the slow Triton journey inward, to capture 60% of that trailing nitrogen and transport it in faster tanker ships to insert into the then much thinner atmosphere of Venus.

After inserting ice asteroids into Venus, Oxygen will also be converted from carbon dioxide to begin the introduction of oxygen into the Venus atmosphere.

The Triton Moon should arrive in the year of approximately 2860.

After Triton is inserted in orbit around Venus, phase three of the ROV project will be put into operation in the year of 2861.

Here again now is Professor Omagus to give you the details of the spin up Process of Planet Venus after all of this has been completed.

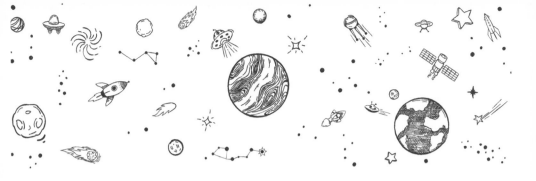

CHAPTER 8
Phase 3
Why Triton was Chosen

Professor Omagus stepped forward again with a round of applause from the audience.

Firstly he began, we need to explain why we chose Triton for the Venus Moon instead of any other potential candidate. So here are some facts about Triton that may not be known to some here.

Triton is the largest moon of Neptune. It was discovered in the year 1846 by astronomer William Lassell. Triton is the only known moon in the solar system with a retrograde orbit. That means it orbits in the opposite direction that the Planet Neptune rotates on its axis.

History surmises that Triton was once a rogue body that was captured by Neptune as it entered the solar system. Possibly a collision with another ice moon even caused the rings that Neptune displays.

Triton is 2710 kilometers or 1680 miles in diameter. Its gravity is only 8% of Earth's and smaller than Earth's Moon and we astronomers consider it the perfect size body to be inserted in orbit of Venus.

Because of its retrograde revolve of Neptune and composition similar to Pluto, it is assumed to be a dwarf planet captured from the Kuiper belt.

In the Voyager 2 flyby in the year 1989, it was discovered that its surface consisted of mostly frozen nitrogen with a percentage of water ice below the surface.

It was ascertained in those days that below that was a rocky surface with a substantial metal core that is tidally locked to Neptune as it revolves retrograde to Neptune's spin once every 5.6 earth days.

Surface temperatures recorded by Voyager 2 in those days were measured to be extremely cold at -235 degrees C and that equals to -391 degrees below zero Fahrenheit.

It is postulated that in three and a half billion years or so if left unchanged, Triton will approach too close to Neptune's Roche limit and be torn apart by gravitational forces.

Triton is also know to be one of the few moons in the solar system to be geologically active and sublimating nitrogen into its atmosphere from active geysers.

Triton's surface has very few impact craters. Its atmospheric pressure is less than one percent of earth's pressure.

Voyager 2 only was able to map about 40 percent of the surface in its long ago rapid flyby.

Triton was named in 1880 after the Greek sea god Triton the son of Poseidon.

Triton's retrograde orbit is already closer to Neptune than Earth's Moon is to Earth. Like I said earlier that in 3.6 billion years from now, Triton will pass within Neptune's Roche limit. That day will result in a collision or break up of the moon and possibly cause a ring system similar to the planet Saturn.

So, Omagus began concluding his lecture on Triton's history and properties. Rightly, we are also rescuing Triton from a far away future catastrophe and using it to help stabilize the Planet Venus.

With that said, I now call to the front to explain phase three of ROV that is scheduled to begin in 2861 an esteem scientist, Doctor Jessica Gulasky

More ovations occurred as Jessica approached the lectern to began her summary of the planned phase three ROV Project

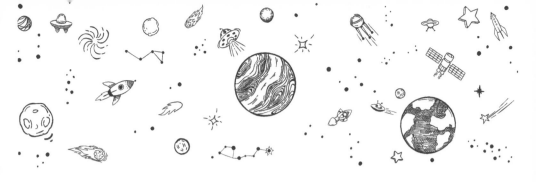

CHAPTER 9

Jessica Gulasky
Phase 3 of ROV

Hello I'm Jessica Gulasky and I'm here to tell you about Phase 3 of ROV that should begin around the year 2861.

Once Triton is placed into a stable Venus orbit in Phase 2, We will soon begin the process of speeding up the rotation rate of Planet Venus.

Since Triton is placed in it's orbit that process alone will have caused Venus to reverse its poles and begin rotating slowly counter clockwise. Triton itself will have caused Venus' rotation speed to have increased slightly but nowhere near enough to cancel its slow spin and long solar days.

Firstly in phase three, Humanity will begin with a fleet of R-A equipped ships to be employed to begin the rotation rate spin up by applying equal but opposite force below the surface equator of Venus on both sides in simultaneous pulses.

A fine tuned 15 percent three second powerful repulse beam will be focused on Venus' iron core from both sides of the equator in opposite directions continuously every earth hour for a total of ten earth years. The end plan is to speed Venus' rotation rate up to spin once every twenty four hours similar to Earth's rotation.

Once Venus has gained similar earth rotation speed its magnetosphere will have engaged to protect the surface from harmful solar radiation.

This speed up is being done gradually to allow Venus to acclimate slowly to the rotation rate increase.

In the beginning, Venus is rotating so slowly that a fast walking pace walking west away from sunrise and never see the sun's position change at early dawn. It rotates counter clockwise in the beginning at a spin rate of approximately seven miles per hour.

Ten earth days combined repulse rate from R-A ships will cause the rotation rate to increase only by one mile per hour for each 10 earth days repulse time.

The total speed increase rate after ten years of R-A pulses, will bring Venus' rotation rate up to approximately one thousand miles per hour.

An esteem scientist from the immediate audience interrupted Professor Gulasky with a question about Triton's long journey and what the facts were about the time it would take to bring the rouge Neptune moon to Venus.

Great question she retorted.

Here are the planned details.

Firstly, Neptune is approximately 2,898,300,000 miles away from planet Venus. That is indeed a great distance. In words that's two billion, eight hundred ninety eight million, three hundred thousand miles.

So, in order to transport Triton to Venus over a 15 year time span, Triton would have to made to have an approximate travel rate of 6.12 miles per second average speed. There's 5475 earth day rotations in 15 years.

That means that Triton will have to cover a distance in one earth rotation of 529,370 miles per 24 hours. So when we divide that number by 24 hours in a rotation, we come up with a speed of approximately 22,058 miles per hour.

If we divide that number by 60 we get a speed of 367.6 miles per minute. One more division by 60 gives us a speed of 6.12 miles per second.

So, that's the speed that Triton will have to continuously travel in order to make it to Venus in 5475 days or approximately 15 earth years time.

Triton itself is traveling approximately 1.5 miles per second in its orbit speed around Neptune. Triton travels 30% above and below Neptune's equatorial ecliptic as it journeys retrograde to the fast rotation of Neptune.

Once every 5.8 Earth days, Triton completes its revolve journey orbit around Neptune of a total distance of approximately 780.000 thousand miles travel in one orbit.

Triton is tidally locked to Neptune and always keeps the same face towards Neptune as it makes one single orbit.

Professor Gulasky began her conclusion statements with a few words of wisdom of her own.

This worthy project called ROV or Revival of Venus, is the most massive project that humankind has ever undertaken. I professor Gulasky, predict that this worthy colossal project will be accomplished in 50 or 60 years time and by that time, she concluded with passionate retort, Planet Venus will be beginning to be habitable for humans to live upon its surface.

That's the ultimate long term goal here. To create another planet similar and near to Earth to help relieve Earth of its over 50 billion humankind overpopulation.

The outer bases and Mars cities are supporting a few thousand souls but we know that earth's population will increase by billions in future centuries and Planet Venus once revived, will only be a 44 day journey at opposition away at Earth's escape velocity of 7 miles per second.

It's just the logical thing to do for future generations to set our goal this day to immediately begin this worthy task of ROV.

Thanks to the discovery of ARAE, Our fleet of ships are equipped and ready to begin the ROV project as soon as this Astronomy Council votes this very day.

Vote they did in a landslide election vote. The vote was unanimous to begin ROV in the immediate future. Earth's population had grown to dangerous levels and in 50 years or so, if Venus is not revived the population of Earth would have exploded even further.

It was 2826 before the ROV Project got into full swing and began their dispatching of R-A equipped ships to begin the process of removing Venus' excess atmosphere.

These R-A tug ship brigades consisted of three squadrons of 15 ships each to handle several stages of the project as it became necessary in the 60 year long ROV project.

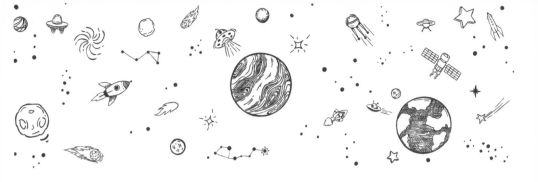

CHAPTER 10
July 29th, 2826
Phase One Begins

The first brigade squadron of 15 tug ships were launched towards Venus to begin the process of thinning the atmosphere of Planet Venus.

Venus was at it's nine o'clock orbital position inside Earth's orbit that day that the brigade one was launched.

Brigade one will arrive coasting at Venus in 44 earth days and immediately orbit the planet and take up their control positions approximately 500 kilometers or 310.6 miles in orbit above Venus. That's just above the top of Venus' thick atmosphere.

That same day squadron team two and three were launched in the direction that Neptune would be in its orbit in a few years time.

As soon as those 30 ships arrive at Neptune, they will begin the set up of an immediate base around Triton that would take nearly six month's preparation before Triton will be stolen away from Neptune's gravity well and begin its 15 year journey towards Venus.

Upon arrival at Venus, Brigade One will lock three of their triangle fifty meter length sides together and be used as a control base station to monitor the process of the other 12 ships in beginning the process of eliminating volatile gasses out of the hot planet's atmosphere.

Each ship in each brigade had fifteen humans aboard to begin the biggest project ever attempted by humanity. The Revival of Venus.

September 30 2826, Fifteen arrow head triangle ships approached Venus' gravity well in a straight line at a slowed speed of 18,000 miles per hour.

Three of the center ships broke away and locked together and departed the line in a specific direction that fell into Venus orbit at 500 miles or 804.6 kilometers above Venus.

Twelve vessels fell in closer just above the top of Venus' 300 mile high atmosphere. Within days, the 12 ships began the process of eliminating the top of the atmosphere with their R-A focused repulse beams.

The repulse beams were focused at a angle so that the unwanted gases were pushed inwards towards the Sun.

As the 12 repulser ships each in their specific orbit vector, each fired a three second blast to the top of Venus' atmosphere focused at first on the high carbon dioxide content.

That process alone would take the next 5 years just to bring down the atmosphere by 20% so the next five year phase could begin.

After 5 years of carbon dioxide removal, Venus is predicted to have it's surface temperature to have cooled down to approximately 500 degrees Fahrenheit. That's predicted to be a good start in the ROV program.

The second 5 year phase, would then focus their efforts on removing the deadly to humans sulphuric acid from Venus' hostile atmosphere.

Fast transporting Nitrogen cargo ships from Tritons inward nitrogen capture journey, would also be introduced into Venus' atmosphere in place of the vicious acid that would be removed and ejected towards the Sun.

After 5 more years of phase 2, the Venus atmosphere's temperature is predicted to have dropped to approximately 300 degrees Fahrenheit on the surface.

Phase 3 will begin as soon as Venus' new Moon Triton is 5 years away in it's journey.

The Venus base station will then begin the process of converted captured carbon dioxide into oxygen and inserting the human necessity gas into Venus' slowly cooling atmosphere.

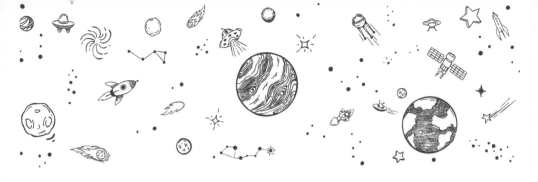

CHAPTER 11

July 27th, 2841
Arrival at Neptune

Two squads of 15 each R-A equipped ships approached Neptune and slowed to proper approach orbit speed.

Compared to Neptune's 30,499 mile fast spinning diameter, Triton appeared tiny ahead as the triangle shaped armada of thirty ships that approached the moon in the opposite direction of Neptune's fast counter clockwise spin.

Here at Neptune, which is indeed the farthest gas giant planet from the sun and at almost 2.8 billion miles from Earth two R-A armed brigades of 15 each began matching Triton's speed and began setting up a base in orbit around Triton for the humongous undertaking ahead.

Six of the thirty ships departed their brigade position and locked together in a higher orbit to form the Triton orbital base station.

Triton Base would be receiving antimatter fuel supply from Earth on a regular scheduled basis and after unloading their fuel supply, the cargo ships would purge their containers and reload with Nitrogen from Triton's atmosphere and haul their gaseous cargo back to supply Venus' atmosphere. Neptune is the smallest of the gas giants.

Mysteriously though, Neptune's gravity is only slightly more than the gravity of Earth. Uranus is much larger in size than Neptune but Neptune contains more mass than Uranus.

Neptune's atmosphere is full of ice clouds that sail around the planet at tremendous speeds. Winds have been measured at 1,300 mph. Neptune's extreme cold temperature has been measured at -367 degrees Fahrenheit

Neptune is the coldest known gas giant in the solar system. Neptune is so cold that any human would flash freeze at that temperature.

Below its cold atmosphere that consist of mostly hydrogen, helium and a little methane, a flash frozen human if still consciously alive would sink into oblivion. Your surroundings would get warmer as you sank lower but a human would never sink to Neptune's postulated rocky core.

Therefore, your forever dead remains would weigh a tiny bit more than it would if the human had died on Earth.

CHAPTER 12

Tritons Escape from Neptune

By the year's end of December 30th, 2842 Triton's retrieval process was in place and ready to remove Triton from Neptune's gravity well.

Twelve R-A equipped ships circled Triton at a fifty degree angle above its equator and twelve more ships circled at 50 degrees angle below the equator of Triton.

Triton was already speeding around Neptune at approximately at 1.6 mps or 2.57 kps.

It was planned that in order to grab Triton from it's orbit, pressure and speed from it's farthest distance from the sun is when the moon would have to be speeded up in its orbital escape velocity of 5.5 mps or a little over 8.8 kps.

From the backside of Neptune, 24 R-A equipped ships will each beamed their powerful repulser at Tritons inner core in order to speed the moon up to the required escape velocity.

In a few earth hours time, Triton will come around Neptune's leading edge as the Moon was now traveling at 5.8 miles per second or 9.3 kps as it slowly pulled away from Neptune's reverse spinning forward revolving grip.

Triton was studiously guided equally by 24 repulse ships and several unloaded fuel tankers that trailed behind the former 6 ships that had detached and followed Triton in preparation to begin the nitrogen capture process that Triton's upper atmosphere was already beginning to trail Triton's forward direction.

Minor quakes were recorded on Neptune as Triton gained enough speed to break Neptune's gravity bond. It was if Neptune was saying goodbye to a long ago captured friend.

Triton sailed it's new path controlled by 24 Repulse Attracter ships and now was speeding along at a continuously set speed of 6.2 miles per second that would take 15 years to arrive near Venus.

It was considered that speeds any faster than that would require Triton to lose too much of it's upper atmosphere at too fast a rate.

So, 6.2 miles or 9.2 kilometers per second, would be the entire speed of the Triton Brigade along the Moon's 15 year captured journey.

Triton now broke away and scattered a trail of Neptune's five fine particle dusty rings.

The Triton moon was held above and below the equator by two brigades of R-A equipped triangle shaped ships.

The repulsive force of 24 R-A ships were required to continuously insert their repulse emitter at equal spaced surface points approximately 50 degrees above and below Triton's equator.

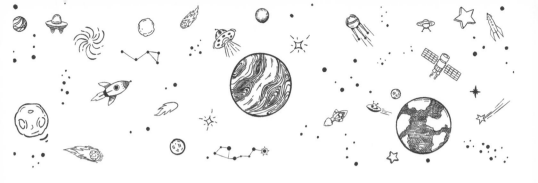

CHAPTER 13
February 16th, 2858
Halfway Point

Now at the halfway point of Tritons transfer, for almost 7.5 years, Triton had sailed escorted inward without incident at a continuous rate of 6.2 miles per second.

Regular antimatter fuel cargo barges were received from Earth to supply the entire inbound operation with the much needed antimatter hydrogen energy pellets and positive helium three pellets required to power the ship's R-A pulse emitters

Once emptied of their cargo fuel, these barges demagnetized and purged into space and then the barges were refilled with the nitrogen that was escaping and captured from the top of Triton's atmosphere as it sailed through the vacuum of space with it's brigade of controlling escorts.

The barges would then be fast shipped inward at ten times the speed of the Triton Brigade's progression through space that was still over 7.5 years away from Venus.

At a speed of 60 mps, the return nitrogen loaded cargo ships could arrive at Venus' vicinity in approximately 10 months time from the half way point of the Triton journey.

Later on, there was indeed one example of a serious mishap when the Brigade was 5 years away from arrival.

One of the ARAE powered ships had malfunctioned and had to be quickly replaced by one of the six ships that was trailing the procession which originally had been one of the six that made up the base station before Triton was originally captured.

It was a necessity that all 24 repulser tugs maintain specific balance of Triton at all times.

Four of the relief ships would relieve a team of two 24 repulse tugs on a regular basis so that the two of the pushers at a time could depart the sequence in order to refuel at the trailing magnetic antimatter storage barges that were re-supplied by earth ships on a regular scheduled basis.

Its all about momentum. Six weeks past Jupiter and physics dictates that for every bit of energy you put into an object to gain a certain speed, You're also going to have to use a equal amount of reverse force to slow that object down to a controllable speed.

Weeks past Jupiter's orbit, the strategy of controlling Triton's inward tow speed had changed to begin slowing down Triton's momentum speed. The Brigade sailed on for days above the asteroid belt and in several more months sailed past Mar's orbit without incident.

In three more months the Earth will be on the opposite side of the sun when the controlled Triton Brigade crosses the earth's orbital path.

By then, the entire Brigade's speed will have decreased to approximately 5 miles per second and stronger reverse pressure would be applied to begin a vigorous reverse attempts to slow Triton down to obtain a 180 degree trailing Venus slow approach from behind orbit.

Planet Earth was on the far side of the Sun when the Triton Brigade crossed its orbit. The Brigades were continuing to change the speed of Triton as it was now 26 million miles away from a Venus orbit.

The projected future path was to have Triton approach Venus from behind the planets almost perfect circular orbit.

Safely past Earth now it was well known that Venus orbits the Sun at a fast speed of 21 miles or 33.7 kilometers per second. That's approximately 78,337 miles per hour.

It was now the Brigade's job to speed Triton up to 21.5 mps in order to slowly approach Venus from behind and have it capture Triton when it was released at the proper time to obtain orbit.

It was also well known that when the 24 brigade approached within a million miles or so of it's destination, that Venus would start its pole reversal to begin for the first time in eons it's new slow eastward rotation.

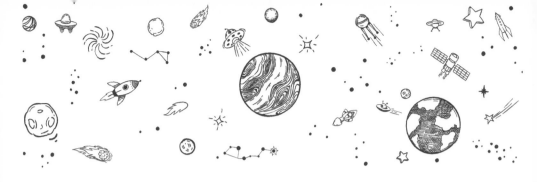

CHAPTER 14

Four Million Miles to Venus

Four million miles away and propulsion was being provided that has increased Triton's speed again to 79,600 miles per hour. Even at a distance of four million miles, it will take another ten months before Triton could catch Venus and then could be inserted into orbit around Venus.

That means that Triton was slowly approaching Venus and gaining on its orbit at speed of 1,263 miles per hour or .35 mps.

At that catch up speed, arrival behind Venus would occur in about ten months time from the four million miles yet to be traveled.

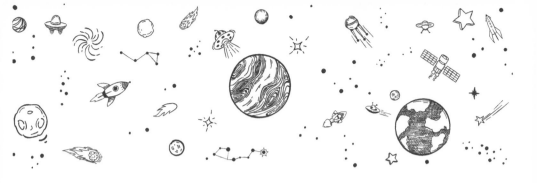

CHAPTER 15
Back at Venus and the Fourth Brigade

Back at Venus, another brigade of 15 ships had been added in preparation for the arrival of the Triton Moon just months away.

Brigade 4 would co-operate with Brigade 1 and take control once Triton had been inserted into a stable orbit around Venus.

It was July 1st 2857, as The Triton Brigade approached within a million miles above and behind Venus.

In 32 more days, the Moon would arrive at its finale destination.

Planet Venus was now feeling the gravitational effects of the approaching from behind Triton moon.

It was predicted that within a half million miles from behind Venus, Triton's gravity will cause Venus to reverse its poles and begin rotating slowly eastwards.

It was an amazing thing to watch on that August 1st 2857 to watch the planet Venus roll over in a 24 hour period as gracefully as a floating giant white cork in a pitch black ocean.

Humans weren't playing God at all. In actuality, the humans of the day were using their technology to fight Planet Earth's 50 billion and still growing overpopulation.

Humankind needed a new world that was close by to relieve its burdensome population explosion. Humankind was still years away from totally teraforming Planet Venus.

Venus was now only two weeks away from moon insertion.

Venus' atmosphere had already been reduce to 1,500 millibars and surface features of brown and green could be seen through its much thinner atmosphere.

Its surface temperature was down to a hot tropical 135 degrees Fahrenheit and more oxygen and nitrogen were being introduced to the atmosphere daily. Very few traces of sulphuric acid could be found now but at higher elevations the danger still existed.

Now is when all the hard work really begins.

CHAPTER 16
Triton's Orbit Insertion

September 12th, 2857

Ever so near to journey completion, Brigade 2 and 3 approached the point of handover to Brigades 1 and 4 to take control and give Triton the exact speed and vector to obtain a proper Venus orbit of approximately 220,000 miles above Venus.

Triton was now traveling at a speed of 2,100 miles per hour around Venus.

Venus' orbital speed around the sun is 78,337 mph so the total speed to obtain orbit means the entire total hand off speed would be made at 80,437 miles per hour in front of Venus' orbital path. That means they were traveling a little over 22 miles per second when the Triton Moon handoff occurred.

It was indeed a remarkable visual site to observe as brigades 2 and 3 handed off the Triton Moon like a huge ball game in space as 1 and 4 captured Triton and guided it towards it's exact vector for Venus orbit insertion.

Triton was inserted into a slightly lower orbit than Earth's moon was because of the smaller 1,600 mile diameter.

Approximately 220,000 miles above Venus Triton was also tidally locked in orbit to always present the same face towards Venus like the Earth's Moon does to Earth.

CHAPTER 17
Venus' Rotation Speed Up

It had been about 32 years since the ROV project had begun and now the long term goal would soon start the process of speeding up Venus' rotation slowly while the atmosphere was still being slowly fined tuned to support human life in Venus' future days.

In order to speed the rotation of Venus up, it had to be done slowly. Triton was now in a 26 day orbit around Venus and it was calculated that the Venus rotation rate speed up would take 30 years or so to accomplish the near 24 hour rotation rate as Planet Earth has.

Since the Triton Moon had been inserted, Venus now rotated eastward at about 8 miles per hour. The Triton Moon's orbit had caused Venus to speed up slightly by almost 1 mph.

ARAE repulser ships for the next 30 years had to speed Venus' rotation rate up very slowly by pulsing Venus' iron core with measured precision pulses.

In order to speed Venus up to Earth rotation speed, in a 24 hour period the pulses would only speed Venus up by a little less than a tenth of a mile per hour per Earth day.

Venus was 81 percent as massive as the Earth is and the slow speed up process would only speed it's rotation rate up by a little over a mile per hour in 10 earth rotations.

In order to simulate earth's 1024 mph rotation speed, the entire spin up process of Planet Venus would take the next 30 years to complete.

Venus had to be sped up slowly to allow its inner iron core after fifteen years or so to begin emitting a protective Van Allen type belt like the one that protects humans from harmful radiation on Planet Earth.

It is also predicted that when the magnetic Van Allen belt has engaged from Venus' sped up rotating core, that the Triton Moon's orbit will cause Venus' rotation axel tilt of approximately 21 degrees and begin to cause seasons on Venus.

By October 2nd. 2873, Planet Venus was now rotating approximately 512 miles per hour.

Frozen captured water ice burgs had steadily been injected into the atmosphere near the poles over the years.

Planet Venus' atmosphere was now opaque and two shallow oceans of green water could be seen from orbit surrounding higher elevation land masses.

Millibars at surface level had decreased considerably and was only 10 percent higher than Earth's at sea level.

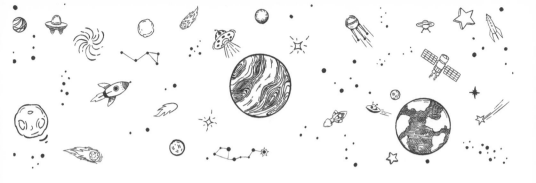

CHAPTER 18
Early Venus Settlers

By now, early settlers had began setting up bases on the still too hot for humans without a spacesuit surface.

Venus before ROV began, was once 960 degrees Fahrenheit and under extreme atmosphere crushing pressure but in 2874, the planet had cooled to an average of 120 degrees Fahrenheit.

Ninety percent of the deadly sulphuric acid had been removed from the atmosphere and the oxygen content was now up to 17 percent.

Nitrogen content had increased to 65 percent but the carbon dioxide was still too high at 12 percent. Other trace gases of argon were also detectable.

Clouds of hot rain covered areas on the globe and Venus had began turning into a beautiful light blue green white world, with a red tinted moon named Triton reflecting sun light towards Venus' night side.

By 2876 The extra mass of Triton added to Venus' mass, had caused Venus to orbit the sun further out at almost 69 million miles distance from the Sun.

The ROV Project had taken a little longer than expected and had progressed steadily for fifty one years and even at 15 years away from completion, Venus glistened blue green in it's new orbit with its rosy Triton Moon.

Surface colonist were already setting up bases in pressurized research stations. For the first time ever astronauts were able to explore the surface of Venus in spacesuits.

From the surface looking up from the night side sky, you could see a lot of rosy colored vapor clouds but every now and then there was a clearing that allowed the stars to shine through.

Their were many steamy hot daylight storms that were always producing 100 degree steamy rain.

Ships were always injecting icebergs towards both poles. Planet Venus was beginning to glisten frosty white at its growing colder poles.

The AERA ships still surrounding Venus and were gradually day by day speeding up the planets rotation.

In this present year of 2877, Venus was rotating once every 48 hours with it's rosy moon Triton completing one tidally locked orbit around Venus every 13.5 Venus rotations or once every 27 Earth days.

There wasn't much need for precision clocks.

Venus clocks weren't set up yet because every 10 earth days, The R-A repulser ships had sped Venus' rotation rate up by another 1 mph.

No clocks could ever stay right with the rotation speed always changing. That would be accomplished once Venus was rotating near earth rotation speed in seven more years.

Venus' Van Allen shield was now doing a nice job producing protection from solar radiation.

It's poles displayed colored borealis much like the poles of Earth.

Numerous lightning sprouts could be seen everywhere from orbit. Planet Venus was slowly acclimating to it's new properties and Triton moon in orbit.

With a few delays all had gone as expected so far. Now, only the last 15 years of ROV remained to be completed.

2878 through 2889

In 2878, colonist were being sent to Venus by a thousand settlers each year. Venus was not yet suitable for humans to be on the surface without a spacesuit but exploration and buildings were being erected in Venus style surface structures.

Farmers in spacesuits now drove huge tractors and plowed Venus' warm soil. Pressurized bases were set up in a grid like pattern. By the year 2879, many plants from earth's tropics had began to flourish and turn the dusty soil into green plants.

Plants love carbon dioxide and Venus had plenty. Plants give off oxygen and Venus needed it so that one day in the future, humans wouldn't need spacesuits to live freely on Venus' surface.

By 2879, Construction crews were hard at work building tar paved roads with magnets below the tarred surface to repel or attract the new magnetic bottom air tight Venusmobiles that had recently began to make the scene of the early explorer population of several thousand humans from Earth.

Two major city settlements had begun and the population of each was approximately three thousand. Venus' surface temperature was gradually getting cooler with the years of teraforming.

Suddenly there was a huge settlement rush in 2880 and two more thousand souls quickly transferred to Venus.

CHAPTER 19

Galena Gold on Venus

It had somehow leaked out over earth's news media that a new type very valuable Venus gold had been discovered in the high altitude mountains north of a new settlement named Pandora that existed half way up Maxwell Montes.

Pandora station was half way up the 11 kilometer tall mountain called Maxwell Montes on Venus at an elevation of almost 16,000 feet.

The atmosphere was thinner there and many new astronaut settlers were arriving to the early settlement base by the hundreds each Venus week.

Fortune seekers from Earth were coming in droves to explore the higher elevation of Maxwell Montes and Aphrodite Terra to capture the new valuable gold of the day substance called lead sulfide.

Near the 35,000 feet elevation of Maxwell Montes and Aphrodite Terra, the atmosphere at that altitude was almost earth-like. Temperature and pressure at that elevation was bearable with out a spacesuit for 30 minute periods.

What was more valuable than gold on Planet Venus, was the lead bismuth or Galena as the miners called it that existed near the very top of Maxwell Montes 6.8 mile high attitude.

Silver Venus Snow that is called lead bismuth was the new fortune seeking substance. With the cooling of Venus, this substance had to be captured and contained before Venus' high elevation atmosphere became too thin.

Helicopter air ship mining crews were making daily sojourns to the top of Maxwell Montes where silver lead bismuth existed. They called it Galena Gold.

Galena was even heavier than earth gold. One single ounce of Galena was worth 10 million dollars at this time in history.

In order to explore and capture this very rare substance that had turned to metal over many eons, mining crews would store it in Venus former pressure and temperature containers.

Galena had super electrical properties like no other metal known. A one centimeter strand of Galena wire could carry as much current as a nuclear fusion reactor could produce.

Lead bismuth or Galena, was indeed a very valuable resource that was the cause of many explorers coming to Venus to gain quick wealth.

The Venus colonies had a base at 16,000 feet altitude called Venus station one. It was here that the first settlers began their first Venus colony at Aphrodite Terra and where the first Galena was discovered high on top of the Aphrodite mountain.

Bladed Helicopter type airships worked well in the Venus atmosphere due to the heavier air pressure. At higher altitudes it was almost becoming Earth-like with a view of the still steamy smoldering valleys below.

Tritons reflected light cold be seen reflecting solar rays from the day and night side of Venus.

Tritons thin nitrogen atmosphere showed hazy red around its rim unlike Earth's Moon with no atmosphere.

All through 2881, thousands more explorers came to Venus to try their luck at mining this lucrative sliver metal named Galena.

Planet Earth had no metal that was this unique and extremely valuable.

This type of Galena metal weighed 30 percent more than gold on Earth and Venus had only about 83 percent Earth gravity.

All in all, things were proceeding well as Venus was going through the last seven years of its revival process.

It had always been called earth's sister planet and now it was becoming a planet much like Earth in its finale years of revival.

There were also many Mars citizens departing Mars to head for Venus and attempt to get in on the Venus Galena riches.

It was an exciting season for all but there were deaths and mishaps that happened due to ill equipped miners that didn't have the proper tools and resources to climb the highest peaks on Venus.

Many tried to climb the highest peaks without airships and died trying to climb impossibly steep cliffs. Mountain climbing on Venus was like trying to climb three times the height of Mt. Everest on Earth. It wasn't just men that came to explore. Many females came as explorers as well to try their luck.

Husbands and wives lived in pressurized tents with portable oxygen tanks that had to be replenished with machines that created oxygen from the upper atmosphere near the tops of the two mining mountains called Maxwell Montes and Aphrodite Terra.

Although Venus' atmosphere had cleared up a lot, traces of sulphuric acid still remained in the atmosphere and spacesuits were always required to navigate the 11 kilometer or 6.8 mile altitude mining site near the top of Maxwell Montes.

Pressure at that altitude was just a little over Earth sea level millibars and temperature at that altitude had dropped to 100 degrees Fahrenheit.

The atmosphere was almost breathable but no chances were taken to possibly encounter traces of the remaining sulphuric acid that would kill a human instantly if breathed.

In the year of 2881, The R-A ships were still repulsing the core of Venus and Venus was now rotating at approximately 803 mph and the Triton Moon sailed along a at 26 earth day revolve around Planet Venus.

The axis of Venus was now tilted 18 degrees to the ecliptic. New Venus was getting more Earth-like by the year. Almost 10 years remained to finish the teraforming process.

Venus misty atmosphere showed the surface features from orbit of two oceans and green plant life that was able to be discerned through hazy white clouds.

Plants were producing sufficient oxygen and nitrogen was still being introduced by cargo tankers that were still collecting the nitrogen from the Triton Moon in orbit. That year was also the beginning of ozone being added to the upper level of Venus' atmosphere.

Several Volcanoes were still very active and omitting hot noxious carbon dioxide gas but their emission had dropped substantially over the past five earth years. Strong Venus quakes were occurring as the planet acclimated to the repulsion of its hot core being speeded up by 1 mph every 10 Earth days.

The diameter of Venus' now had a bulge at the equator that would increase even more before the teraforming of Venus was completed.

Presently, a year on Venus took approximately 270 earth days to orbit the Sun once. The extra two million miles distance further from the Sun was defiantly the cause of that and the new Venus year.

Venus at opposition to the Earth-Moon system was a little over 24 million miles distance from Planet Earth. That's approximately 88 times the distance that our Moon is to Planet Earth.

In the Earth year 2882 strange happenings began to occur that no one had ever expected.

Venus' gravity suddenly had decreased by 3 percent due to the centrically increase of the planets rotation rate change.

Scientist discovered that Venus was developing continental plate shift and land masses were separating by .05 inches per Venus year.

The planets rotation rate was now 851 mph at the equator. The three percent gravity loss due to centrifugal force, was not considered a major problem but for every 100 Earth pounds that you would weigh on Earth, You would now weigh 83 pounds on Venus.

Due to that unexpected gravity loss, the Triton Moon had increased its distance from Venus by approximately a thousand kilometers or 620 miles.

Immediate action by a dozen repulser ships had to be dispatched in order to immediately begin adjusting Triton's orbital speed. If no changes were ever made to Triton's orbital speed, the Moon would one day soon leave its orbit of Venus. It took about six earth months to rectify the situation.

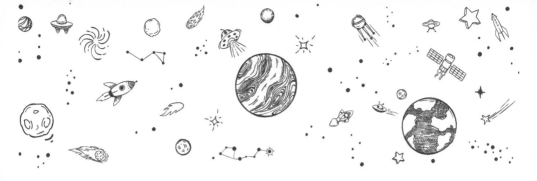

CHAPTER 20
Anunnaki Intervention

March 13th, 2883

It came across the news media that morning that 8 unknown ships had entered the edge of the solar system. They were unknown crafts that were headed towards the inner solar system at a tremendous speed.

An armada of 12 Earth military ships were dispatched to investigate and intercept the incoming unknown vessels.

The encounter occurred just inside Neptune's orbit as 12 Earth ships met the huge unknown 8 alien vessels. The eight alien ships dwarfed the Earth ships in size. On single alien vessel was larger than all 12 of the Earth military vessels.

Just as 12 more Earth ships appeared in assistance to the first 12 ships, the alien vessels engaged a sort of barrier that surrounded their 8 humongous ships.

24 Earth military ships appeared tiny but stood nose to nose with the eight large alien unknown vessels. Stand off minutes passed but no communication was conducted between either race.

All the earth military ships knew of the present situation was that our solar system had been invaded by eight giant unknown alien ships that had halted their progress and sat silently before the much smaller 24 Earth ships.

All at once, the 24 Earth ships were pushed aside by some force and the alien ships resumed their course towards the inner solar system.

The twenty four ships regained control and began pursuing the alien vessels.

Suddenly one of the ships broke formation and challenged the Earth vessels.

Strong vibrations were felt as all earth vessels launched a repulser beam that didn't seem to affect the ship at all.

The alien ship just sat there blocking the way as the other seven continued their inward journey towards the inner solar system.

Suddenly the huge ship projected a wide beam of its own towards the 24 earth ships and they all were flung furiously towards the outer solar system. The repulser beams that were strong enough to move worlds seemed to have no effect what so ever on the one alien ship that had blocked their path.

Only half of the earth ships had survived and were able to recover from the beam that they were hit with from the one alien ship. The one huge ship had swatted the entire brigade of military earth ships like they were annoying insects.

In the meantime the one alien ship had turned and resumed its course to follow the other seven alien vessels. All the remaining earth ships could do at this point was to head inward again and warn the officials on Earth and Venus of their situation and resume their course and try to catch the alien vessels headed towards their home worlds.

At the rate these eight vessels were moving, they would arrive at Planet Earth in about 12 hours time with the remaining armada of 12 ships that were following would then arrive 6 hours behind the immanent invasion.

These beings were extremely powerful. Whom ever they were, they were indeed a powerful force to be reckoned with.

Planet Earth had received the communication from their remaining armada and had set up hundreds of ships just behind the Moons orbit and awaited the incoming large ship's confrontation.

Their had been no communication from incoming huge alien vessels and no one had any idea of what to expect when they arrived.

The aliens arrived at Earth with a assumed furry of evil intentions. All Earth ships were paralyzed upon their arrival and were unable to do anything to stop this incursion. All earth-wide broadcast were interrupted by a picture of an on screen dubious symbol of a pyramid with a tall human likeness crossed out in its center.

The world waited for an explanation as the 8 ships orbited at three hundred miles above the Earth's atmosphere.

24 silent hours passed before a response from the ships came.

We are Anunnaki. We ruled humankind here well over 5,000 of your earth years ago. When we left this system in those days, we had set up a society of peaceful goals that you earthlings have now upset the course of natural events of the planet that you refer to as Venus.

From this day forth we the Anunnaki forbid further changing of your neighbor world Venus until your leaders hear the reason.

Venus was the way it was because the Creator of the universe intended it to be as it was and not the way you have attempted to make it.

We Anunnaki are the messengers of the Almighty. We Anunnaki were sent here as a messenger by the Creator of all to temporally rectify this situation.

We the Anunnaki will land our vessels near the pyramids of ancient Egypt and a council of world leaders will convened with a demand that all earth members attend in that location in 30 of your earth revolutions.

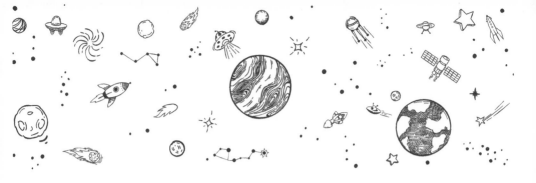

CHAPTER 21
Worlds in Shock and Worry

The worldwide broadcast from the Anunnaki ended in silence as abruptly as the message had started.

The worlds were in shock and worry. Humankind was helpless against any confrontation of such powerful beings.

The United Nations had immediately called upon all world leaders to see what could be done about this sudden response to the ROV Venus project that was 90% completed.

The first United Nation human council meeting began at 6 AM on March 15th, 2883.

An angry Russian delegate stood up first with a mean response. We should fight these Anunnaki he stated emphatically. They claim that they have been sent here by the Almighty and yet we have no evidence of that. We should never be dictated to by aliens.

Perhaps they have a good reason for their actions other than being directed by the Almighty to do so the China delegate spoke next. We should candor our response until all the details are presented at their meeting in Cairo Egypt in 28 days.

The North Korea delegate stood up with a snarled look upon his face. We not allow any being to enter our country and dictate their morals upon us. We not believe in God anyway. We shall fight.

Then your nation and all your citizens may be destroyed the USA delegate responded.

No care responded upset North Korea delegate. We fight we never surrender. We destroy with Nukes he sat down angrily.

It's way too early for that responded the US delegate. We all need to stay calm until the details are presented at their Council meeting.

Nothing is to be gained by starting a war before we hear the facts.

We have Nuclear weapons the North Korea delegate stood again and shook his fist towards the ceiling. We destroy invaders.

The North Korea delegate just snarled an ugly face towards the US delegate and sat firmly back in his seat once more.

The Turkey delegate directed his response towards North Korea. Nuclear weapons are a thing of the past he stated firmly. Since the R-A discovery, hardly any nation depends on their defense response in that category anymore. These powerful Anunnaki would probably laugh at such an attempt. We need to stay calm.

Then the North Korea delegate seemed to grow even more angry.

He stood again and called all the members attending cowards and stormed out of the room. We fight till death, he spoke in broken English as his departing loud words echoed through the large United Nation chamber.

Japan, Egypt and other world leaders spoke up and agreed that caution and patience was the way to approach this serious issue that had been imposed unexpectedly upon all nations of Planet Earth and Venus and Mars Cities.

The deciding vote with the exception of North Korea, was unanimously decided to stay calm and wait for the Anunnaki Council meeting that was to occur 28 days from the first emergency meeting's conclusion.

In the meantime, two of the alien huge Anunnaki vessels were stationed above Venus and the ROV project had been put temporally on hold.

Except for the incident near Neptune's orbit, no attack was made upon any Earth vessels and several more United Nation meetings took place that ended with the same conclusion as to wait and see what will happen at the upcoming Anunnaki council meeting scheduled to take place at 8 am April 13th, 2883 in Cairo Egypt.

Several weeks past by and there had been no further communication received from the Anunnaki to any Nation. All leaders of Earth waited and anticipated further communication from the Anunnaki. Then suddenly on April 9th, the worlds communication network was interrupted by the Anunnaki and this message was broadcast to the entire Planet Earth population.

In four rotations of Earth, all leaders of all nations will convene before our council in Cairo Egypt. There will be no exceptions allowed. The message was short but was continually broadcast for 48 hours without interruption.

All of the nation's leader and its people did not know what to expect but with due process all had agreed to attend. That is, with the exception of North Korea's leader. His stubbornness would indeed test the Anunnaki orders but he personally would have to answer for his actions.

A nervous planet awaited. At this point, no one was even sure of what these Anunnaki beings looked like. All anyone had to go on was ancient Earth's vague details of exactly how large they were and what there appearance would be.

Once the Anunnaki had landed six of their huge vessels, all of Cairo Egypt had been surrounded by a force field that no one could see through or enter or leave.

The entire city of Cairo now appeared as a huge domed mile high structure from Earth orbit.

Two days before the Anunnaki council meeting in Cairo, hundreds of tents were set up all around the huge three mile perimeter of the Anunnaki's force field that prevented anyone from seeing what was inside.

Not much was known about the Anunnaki but history tells that they were deities that were originally from Mesopotamia and were exclusively anthropomorphic.

They were thought to posses extraordinary powers. They were also envisioned as being extremely large in physical size compared to humans.

These deities wore a substance called Melam which is an ambiguous substance which covered them in a terrifying splendor.

The effect of seeing a deities Melam has on humans is described as a physical tingling of the flesh.

These deities were always depicted wearing horned caps consisting of up to seven superimposed pairs of ox-like horns. They were also depicted as wearing clothes with elaborate decorative gold and silver ornaments sewed into their garments.

It is written in history that the ancient Mesopotamians believed that they as deities lived in the heavens but their God-like status was a physical embodiment of God himself.

In 2112 BC, the Anunnaki were given constant care and priest would help clothe them and place feast before them so they could eat.

These Anunnaki Gods also had chariots which they used for transportation on land.

As recorded in ancient history, these Anunnaki deities would transport their selves to a location of a battle so that they could watch the battle unfold. That's basically all the information that was known about the Anunnaki by all the members of the United Nations before the upcoming Council meeting of the Anunnaki.

CHAPTER 22

The Anunnaki's Message is Revealed

April 13th, 2883.

Mysteriously, at 7:40 AM Cairo Time on the morning of the scheduled demanded Anunnaki Council Meeting. The Earth shook for ten minutes then from the top of the mile high dome over Cairo a beam of light projected towards the heavens and the walls of the humongous dome that was concealing Cairo began to slowly disappear from the top down.

It took about 20 minutes for the huge dome to dissipate all the way to the ground to reveal a now emerald green Cairo City with seven giant Anunnaki beings standing before a rebuilt coliseum of ancient Roman style.

The seven giant figures stood drabbed in silver and gold garments and standing thirty feet tall in all of their mystical godly splendor.

One Anunnaki stepped forward and raised its giant scepter and spoke in a booming voice translated to all humans at once.

The voice was loud but somewhat feminine as it echoed across the land.

I am Inana the Anunnaki assigned goddess of Venus.

It was almost 4,800 years ago that our home world that you humans refer to as Nibiru, entered this solar system and caused much havoc to many worlds here.

In those long ago days, the Anunnaki were sent to Earth by the Almighty Creator to protect and save as many humans of that day as possible from the coming again of our world Nibiru.

In those long ago days the Anunnaki trained humans to work in stone.

The three pyramids of Gaza were built as protection in preparation of our heavy gravity Nibiru's approach into the inner solar system that caused much havoc at the time.

Those pyramids and others were used as protection shelters to protect many humans. The pyramids protected them from a tremendous amount of fire rock debris that fell from the heavens as our world Nibiru passed inward towards its 5,026 of your years orbit of this star.

Once our world had looped inward and circled the Sun on the way out, We Anunnaki rejoined our planet and have existed there ever since. We came to Earth then to help some humans survive. Over the eons passage of time, the Anunnaki have done this many times to help humans and ourselves survive.

Anunnaki knows now that humans have progressed much in science, physics and astronomy at this point of your existence. That is not about why we have come to Earth this time. This time is about you being incapable of knowing your future and that is the reason that we Anunnaki have returned to Earth now.

Our world Nibiru exist at present way past the edge of your known solar system. It is now well past its apex and in 860 of your Earth years, the Nibiru will return again. We have calculated the precise orbit of our home world Nemesis for eons but this time things are extremely different. With a pause she stated bluntly.

Planet Earth and Nibiru will be destroyed.

Escalated Concerned erupted followed by gasp from some of the Earth leaders attending.

Then all settled down into a whispered silence of fear while returning their attention back towards the thirty feet tall Inana with extreme worry.

Inana's Melam garment effect began tingling the humans back to complete silence as she spoke once again.

It is not the Anunnaki that will destroy Planet Earth. We Anunnaki have many times saved the humans of Earth from close passes of our home world Nibiru.

This time, it is imposed by the Almighty Creator that even We the Omnipotent Anunnaki are incapable of stopping the Earth's Apocalypse and our home world Nibiru's destruction.

In your year of 3740, our world Nibiru will surely collide with Earth. Earth's destruction is imminent and will surly be destroyed on September 13th of that future year.

We the Anunnaki are presently leaving our world Nibiru to survive and embark on a interstellar journey. We are unable to help Earth humans this time due to our own Nibiru's destruction. We Anunnaki must leave our world also to survive.

Humans of Earth should surely listen to this warning. It is now time for humans to begin your planning of your own combined desires to survive the coming destruction of the Nibiru and Earth.

If You succeed in this survival undertaking, It will insure that some beings of human-kind will survive this destruction of your home world Planet Earth and our own Nibiru that is ordained by the Creator of All.

We Anunnaki will not intervene this time. We can not. It is forbidden because we must insure that our own race will survive also.

In conclusion, Our world Nibiru is an extremely dense high gravity world that has a hundred times gravity that the Earth has.

Nibiru is over 30,000 miles in diameter but has a gravity so strong that your repulser emitters will not be able to change its course.

Earth's destruction is unstoppable but human-kinds existence is not. Chose your future actions well. Your own fate is yours to win. You of Earth have been duly warned. In two Earth rotations, We Anunnaki will depart Earth to return to our own survivals future.

Once the destruction of Earth and the Nibiru occurs, for centuries fiery boulders and stones will bombard other worlds also.

Anunnaki implores humans to seek your future with caution and wisdom. It will be 5 years before your astronomy science allows you to verify that Nibiru is coming. We will leave shortly and place this warning in human hands.

As quickly as Inana finished her speech, the dome began reappearing from the ground up and in 20 minutes time Cairo was invisible again.

All of Earth's leaders were shocked at the Anunnaki disclosure of Earth's immanent destruction. It was very apparent now to all that the ROV project was a necessity and their only hope of human survival.

Long range astronomy scientist were attempting to verify exactly where Venus would be in its orbit on that dreadful future day of September 13th, 3740.

Early indications looked promising but none were sure of the finale position Venus would be on that apocalyptic day.

The ROV project was immediately prioritized with the Anunnaki news of Earth's finale future day revealed. It was predicted by many scientist that possibly Venus and its Moon Triton may have to be moved in its orbit also.

Although the Anunnaki had stated that the Nibiru's gravity was too strong for their R-A devices to handle, it was postulated that maybe they will be able to move Venus and Triton if it became necessary. If that was to be the case, it would indeed require thousands of the R-A ships to make it happen.

A week past the Anunnaki departure, the eight ships were recorded leaving the solar system past the orbit of Eris a dwarf planet way past Pluto in the outer solar system.

CHAPTER 23

Eight Hundred Sixty Years to Earth's Destruction

Eight hundred and sixty years seems like a long time but in reality, it's just a tiny grain in the sands of time when you think about it long term.

Venus teraforming itself was far from being completed and even then humans would not be able to walk its lower surface unprotected for hundreds of years.

There would come a day when that was possible if humanity made it so but all in all, humans of Earth really had their work cut out for them to make it happen in the future here on Planet Venus.

Now, humans absolutely had no choice. Neither the Humans or the Anunnaki could change Earth's future destruction.

Immediately in earth's future years, R-A ships were being built by the thousands.

In 2889 Venus was habitable by explorers but still humans of the day had to wear protective space suits to survive the still hot environment.

It was predicted that Venus would not cool down to Earth's temperature for several centuries.

Astronomers had now detected the dreaded Nibiru way past the Kuiper belt on the edge of the solar system. The Kuiper belt is a doughnut shaped debris field that circles the Sun fifty astronomical units past Pluto with one AU being equal to 93,000,000 miles.

That's 4,650,000,000 miles away from Pluto's orbit.

In words, 4 billion 650 million miles.

The Nibiru at that distance only appeared as a single pixel on long range scanners but it was surly headed inward as the Anunnaki had warned. The Nibiru was moving relatively slow at the moment but it's high gravity would in a few years would pick up speed as it headed inward.

Scientist had predicted that this high gravity world Nibiru had a hundred times the gravity of Earth.

The Nibiru world was definitely very condensed and producing powerful gravity effects way out in the Kuiper belt as it drew nearer to the edge of the solar system.

Studious work prevailed by humans for the next five and a half centuries and Planet Venus had become quite Earth-like in appearance but still only about one billion humans lived on Venus in the year 3436.

The Nibiru appeared larger in telescopes but was still 304 years away from Earth's destruction day.

Now with more precise measurements, it was clear that although Venus would not be struck by Nibiru, it's orbit in September 3740 would put the planet in extreme peril of the blasted matter that would occur on the day of Earth's destruction.

Venus and Triton had to be moved in their orbits and that would be no easy task to complete.

It was now precisely calculated by astronomy scientist that the Planet Venus and its new Triton Moon would have to be moved past the 93 million mile Earth orbit to approximately 98 million miles and opposite the Earth's position on the other side of the Sun in order to evade the molten rock matter that would be blasted inward when Nibiru struck Planet Earth on September 13th, 3740.

Still 304 years away, several thousand or so R-A ships began the process of beginning the Venus, Triton relocation adventure. Humans had no choice. It was do or die.

Worldwide disorder had broken out on Earth when the 51 billion population learned that only selected individuals would be allowed to survive the apocalypse of Earth's coming destruction.

There was no such thing as law and order anymore because Democracy no longer existed to the billions that would be left behind.

Many humans of various nations had decided that if they could not be offered the chance to survive, that they would begin attacking Venus with missiles as an act of selfish hatred.

The Nation of North Korea that was the only nation not represented at the Anunnaki Council, had began firing nuclear weapons in the direction of Venus in its attempt to destroy everything that had been accomplished at this point.

R-A ships easily struck the missiles down before they could reach anywhere near present day Planet Venus.

By 3440, thousands of R-A ships lined up around Venus and Triton to begin the Venus and Triton move out past Earth's present orbit. One would think that if moving Venus was possible that moving Earth would be possible also. Certainly that was not the case here at all.

The Anunnaki had said that Earth and Nibiru were being destroyed by the Almighty Creator and that nothing that the humans could do would change that fact or save Earth from destruction.

It was so ordained to happen by the Universe's Creator regardless of any human attempted interaction.

In other Words, You can't compete with God Almighty. Evidently, God had a reason for this action above and beyond humankinds ability to reason or comprehend. At least this fact is true. God Almighty had sent his messengers the Anunnaki to give some humans a chance to survive.

Two hundred more years passed and around 3640 Venus and Triton were moving past Earth's orbit guided by thousands of R-A ships and heading for an assumed safe spot to evade most of the destruction that the Nemesis would cause when it struck Earth in a hundred years.

Even though the Nibiru was still several billion miles away, It appeared as large as the Moon would appear in the night sky on Earth.

Humans could easily discern fiery lightning from it's edges as it proceeded inward way behind Jupiter in its inward travel.

Gravitational effects were being felt already as the ocean waters of Earth rose and fell in unpredictable surges.

Many of the 48 billion that remained on Earth had already perished to death by the violent eruptions of Earth's interior being spewed into the atmosphere. Planet Earth and the Moon still existed but were definitely suffering many ill effects from the coming destructive Nibiru.

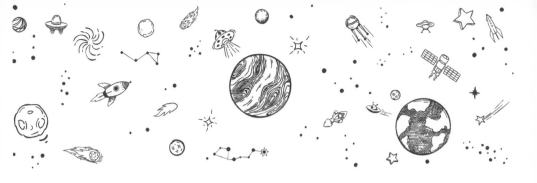

CHAPTER 24

Planet Nibiru Approaches

Earths rotation had ceased and the Moon itself had been ejected way out of its normal orbit of Earth.

Oceans rushed to one side due to the slow rotation that earth now turned and the extreme gravity effect of the approaching Nibiru.

Earth had turned into a frightful place to live on and the few that still survived had lost all hope of any such rescue attempt.

Two billion selected by lottery souls now lived on Venus as the Nibiru grew nearer to Earth by the day. The once beautiful Earth had turned to a dusty red gray circumference as the volcanic dust filled the once breathable atmosphere. Planet Earth was doomed. There are no other words that possibly could describe it. Planet Earth would soon be non existent.

Venus was now in its temporary ninety eight million mile orbit from the Sun with the moon Triton safely tucked in a orbital revolve.

Pointed upward stone pyramids with shelters below on Venus now served as protection from the predicted for years coming of falling hot boulders. Venus citizens were terrified of the coming destruction of their once home world Earth.

No one could even begin to fathom what that day in September 3740 would even be like.

Even on the new Venus, effects were being felt from the gravitational effects of the massive Nibiru that filled the sky of Venus even though Venus was headed for the opposite side of the Sun.

From this distance on Venus, planet Earth was visible equal to a tenth of the size that the Moon once was visible from Earth.

Nibiru also had grown larger in size as it now crossed the opposite side of the orbit of Planet Mars.

Tremendous lightning strikes were easily seen projecting it's powerful bolts inwards towards the Sun's inner system. The entire solar system was in peril. Mars cities had retreated underground to survive the Nibiru Wrath. Venus citizens also had retreated below their pyramid structures in hopes to survive the approaching terrifying Nibiru threat.

When the Nibiru was 20 million miles distance from Earth, Earth was being pulled at its equator and swollen on one side as it had stopped rotating completely and was now being pulled outwards towards the fiery approaching Nibiru's Death grip it was in.

CHAPTER 25

The Earth and Nibiru Collide

September 12th, 3740

The R-A ships had placed Venus and Triton on the opposite side of the sun at a distance of approximately 100 million miles. The explosion from the surface of Venus would not be able to be seen because the Sun would be blocking the view. Satellites were in place to record the apocalyptic event of Earth and Nibiru's finale moments of existence.

September 13th, 3740
819 AM, former Earth eastern standard time

From the surface of Venus on the far side of the Sun, there was a moment that the Sun blinked and produced a sunbow of colors as the explosive compression waves wrapped around the Sun a little over 8 minutes after impact.

It was as if the Sun itself was pushed backwards and closer to Venus by a half million mile due to the Nibiru and Earth's destruction.

CHAPTER 26

Venus Hides Behind the Sun for Protection

Satellite video showed the collision to be as bright as two suns in space for several minutes as much of the matter of the two worlds were evaporated into nothingness after the compression waves had ceased.

Invisible momentarily to the eye, was all of the spewed matter that once made up Earth and the Nibiru that was hidden in the explosive flash.

As the tremendous flashed subsided to half of its original brightness, satellites revealed huge chunks of matter being dispersed in all directions where Nibiru and Earth once existed.

At a time just after the crash, there occurred a giant implosion suction in the area of the collision that echoed throughout the entire solar systems.

Remaining planets rocked in their orbits as the fast moving shock wave passed each in their own turn.

Mars was propelled outward slightly to 142.5 million miles in its orbit and even the mighty Jupiter and other large gas worlds were shaken by the explosion the day that the Earth and Nibiru died.

Some of the matter was ejected towards the Sun at tremendous speeds but much of the hot matter was spewed outward in many other directions.

Planet Venus had missed much of the original percussion wave but its exit orbit behind the Sun placed it in harms way of the rock matter that was skirting the trailing edge of the Sun's Corona.

September 18th, 3740, Planet Venus was struck by thousands of fire lightning boulders from the sky as what was left of humanity trembled underground in their pointed below ground shelters.

Venus quakes larger than any ever felt on Earth continued for several years. The teraforming that had once been almost completed now suffered the wrath of matter that was the remains of Earth and the Nibiru.

The Planet Nibiru had been an enemy of the solar system for eons. Many times human civilizations had lost their past identity and history due to encounters in the solar system when the Nibiru world came inward every 5000 years.

This time the Anunnaki themselves had to flee their world in search of safety and were unable to save humans of Earth from the effects of the Nibiru's collision with Earth.

The Creator had decided that much of the Earth's humans were too corrupt and this time the Nibiru also was to be destroyed so it could never corrupt the solar system ever again.

Planet Venus had turned into a Noah's Ark of the day and humans were given one last chance to survive by their wits without the help of the Anunnaki's intervention.

The Anunnaki as powerful as they were, also had to devise their own futures existence. Their world existed no loner either.

It was assumed by survivors that they had exited this solar system and were destined to find a planet around another star in the Milky Way Galaxy to dwell on.

All In All, September 13th had been a very dreadful time in this now tamed from the Nibiru's destruction of the solar system. The Nibiru would never come again. It was forever eliminated along with Planet Earth.

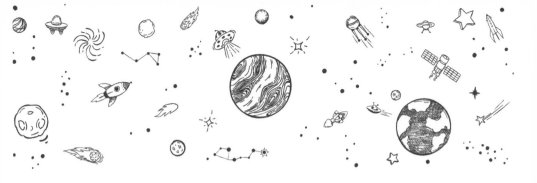

CHAPTER 27
A Hundred and Ten Years Past Nibiru

By the year 3850, humankind of Venus were existing above and below the surface at times. Venus was still approximately 98 million miles from the Sun in its orbit and now had cooled from the immediate bombardment of fire boulders.

Our star the Sun now had a ring of matter surrounding it near the orbit that Venus once existed. The Sun from Venus now appeared like a bright Saturn globe with colored hot rings. Much of the matter had been consumed by the Sun but more than 40 percent of Nibiru and Earth matter now orbited our star at approximately 60 million miles distance.

Of the two billion that fled to Venus, only about One billion of those humans had survived.

It took many months for the shock wave blast to cease and for the entire solar system to somewhat settled down.

The three Mars Cities had barely survived the Nibiru's apocalypse of the destruction of planet Earth and Nibiru. Steadily the humans that survived on Mars began to rebuild their partially destroyed Cities and slowly begin repopulation.

Planet Venus was now pot marked with numerous craters but in the year 3790 the ROV project had finished teraforming the atmosphere and had began moving Triton and Venus inward to an approximate orbit that the destroyed Earth once occupied.

Venus had cooled tremendously in the past fifty years while it occupied it's 98 million mile from the Sun orbit. Fifty two percent of it's surface was now covered with oceans and dust from the volcanoes that spewed magma into the air surrounded the base of several mountains.

As the population began leaving their under pyramid protection shelters, humans could now breathe the air that had been totally changed for human consumption.

On a regular basis, hot boulders still fell from a sky that was now blue. The danger of being struck by a meteor near civilization was no where as bad as it once was in the earlier years.

CHAPTER 28
Celesta and Thomas Explore the New Venus

It is recorded that I Celesta Marcia was born on Venus on New April 25th in the year 3892 and had been raise by my parents Cody and Jeanine Marcia.

In 3912, I had graduated from the only college of Venus entitled New World Academy.

In 3913, I was now employed as an explorer by the Academic Venus Exploration Corporation. In these new days even females could engage in exploration.

I and my partner Thomas Perskipsi, after a year of survival training set out early one Venus morning of November 10th of 3914 to explore the base of the never explored valley of Aphrodite Terra in an exploration rover that was well equipped to handle any Venus situation that we should encounter.

For many long Venus hours, Thomas and I had piloted the rover we called Dependence around steaming hot craters that had been created by falling boulders from the Venus sky.

Just like Noah's Ark, Earth ships had transported many animal species and plant life to the new world in hopes that that they would survive and prosper here as humans were attempting to do.

Far ahead in the distance we spotted a huge herd of Buffalo-like creatures that had gathered near a running water stream at the base of Aphrodite Mountain.

These animals were similar to buffalo but had unique features of there on with purplish mange hair that shimmered in the Venus sunlight and they had pointed single nostril snouts.

As we grew nearer to the herd it was evident that our presence was not welcome by the Venus Buffalo.

There was also a herd of cattle-like critters further on far past the buffalo creatures that we had decided to investigate for the purpose of our scientific journal.

Our Dependence Rover was also a tree seed planter and as the tracks of the rover moved along at 10 mph, it shot a piston into the surface and planted tree seeds as it moved ahead.

Venus' atmosphere was 10 percent thicker than the former Earth's and sound traveled somewhat slower than it once did on Earth.

The piston impacted the surface with a low toned thud as Thomas and I proceeded further ahead in our exploration journey.

Thomas piloted the rover as I dutifully scanned the forward radar to monitor the situation ahead.

Hey, Check this out I insisted to Thomas as he stopped the Rover abruptly and stood to view the long range radar visual.

Wow he exclaimed. What the heck could that possibly be? Both Thomas and I were astounded at what the monitor screen was projecting to us.

It appears to me to be some sort of hump back yellow jelly-like mammals that appear to be mating.

Thomas engaged the rover again and creped along towards the weird animals a mile or so ahead.

In 10 minutes time that were within fifty yards of the yellow hump back jelly creatures that had one eye and three short fat structured legs.

The two creatures wiggled as they appeared to be mating and paid no attention what so ever of our presence.

The frightful sound of thunder was suddenly followed by sharp purple lightning as a storm approached quickly without warning. The creatures immediately scurried away towards an opening in the base on the far side of Aphrodite Terra.

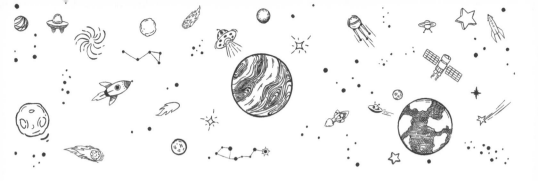

CHAPTER 29

Our First Venus Surface Storm

Black clouds on Venus suddenly let loose with warm liquid rain water quickly filling the shallow crater that the rover had just exited.

Patiently, Thomas and I sat out the steamy down pour that completely obstructed any view that we had before the storm started. Venus winds howled and sharp blue electric lightning struck the ground all around Dependence Rover.

I then reached towards the control panel and quickly engaged a force field around Dependence that quieted the noise of the loud dangerous storm and protected the rover from extreme lightning.

For ten Venus hours we were trapped and unable to travel ahead further until the storm finally subsided just about the time that the Sun was setting in the western Venus sky. We had no choice in the matter. It wasn't safe to proceed.

The rover protected us well but as dusk came on Venus and stars began shinning, it was decided that we should bed down for the night and wait for the dawn to light the way for further exploration.

The Venus night time temperature outside had plummeted to below freezing and the rosy colored Triton Moon lit the surface with pale soft shadows.

Planet Mars was brightly visible to the right of the Triton Moon and many brilliant stars filled the Venus night sky.

There was indeed a very spooky effect that echoed as various Venus animal species bellowed their weird sounds through the long Venus night.

Thomas and I retreated to our separate compartments to get some much needed rest.

Venus time, November 11th, 3915 at 520 AM, Thomas and I were awakened by a sudden loud noise outside our Dependence Rover.

Suddenly the Rover shook violently and almost tilted up on the side and landed with a thud.

Thomas and I were thrown and tumbled to the floor as the rover landed back on it's traction treads. Once again the rover was tossed sideways as we attempted to stand up.

A moment of calm allowed us to scurry to the front to engage the outside monitor. As the front shudders open to reveal the Venus early dawn, off to the right stood a furious looking creature of a fairly large size.

I Celesta quickly engaged the force field to surround the rover as it came charging towards the rover again. The creature was twice the size of an earth elephant and as it charged forward furiously snorting Venus dust below its nostrils and it bellowed a high pitch howl from its one center head huge spiked horn.

The force field energized just as the creature reached its boundary and repulsed and shocked the creature backwards in the air slamming it to the surface upon its back with a ground shaking thud.

The Venus creature slowly regained its stance and quickly exited the scene towards the base of the mountain.

That was close Thomas stated. If you hadn't energized the forcefield in time, the rover might have been crushed by those huge feet that the creature had. Yea I stated with eyes wide open, all six of them. We both expressed a nervous laugh and retreated towards the small galley for an early breakfast snack before duty status.

630 AM November 11th, 3915

This time I Celesta slid into the pilot seat and engaged the rovers slow forward traction tracks to begin our new journey around a crater lake body that led us away from the Mountain base in a westerly direction towards unexplored territory.

Far ahead in the distance their appeared to be a drop off of the terrain that the depth couldn't be determined by radar.

Steady thumps were heard from the piston tree planter as Dependence traversed the 50 kilometer distance in a little over 3 hours time.

I suddenly locked the rover down near the edge of the drop off and engaged the camera boom over the edge to see what was in the deep canyon below.

As the video came into focus there was displayed an unusual scene far below at the bottom of the deep canyon.

Almost 10 kilometers below existed a steamy swirling mass of hot volcanic ash that was swirling down inside Venus in a counter clockwise spin. The canyon itself was half as large as the recorded size of Earth's former grand canyon and it's walled sides were slowly being eroded away from the down swirl of hot air downdraft.

Temperatures down there seem to exceed a thousand degrees Fahrenheit Thomas said. That must be what is left of the ancient Venus' existence. Yea I replied. There's nothing we need to be exploring in that hellish pit. I think we should move on and leave that part of Venus to its own devise.

There appears to be a greenish area ahead to the right at the point of this hot crater. What say we head along this humongous hole and see what's over there. I agree Thomas stated. It's probably going to take us quite a while to get there maybe by sunset we can make it if we try.

Ok I said, we're off to see the wizard or whatever that entails I quipped in jest. There's no need to engage the tree planter because nothing will take root along the edge of the obnoxious gas fumes coming from that hot pit.

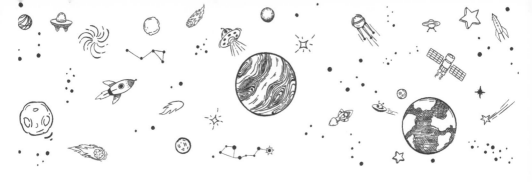

CHAPTER 30

The North Point of The Venus Canyon

Long hours had passed as the rover and crew drove a swerving path all along the craters edge. One Venus null after another the rover continued up and down around the crater slowly nearing the green area that had been spotted from their journey to the edge.

The rover exited the rim and drove a kilometer west as the land had settled down to a flat area between hilly plains.

Another mile to the north displayed a group of plants like none ever seen before. There was no wind at the moment but the green weird plants seemed to dance back and forth as if they were reaching skyward through cloud shielding sunlight.

The weird plants swayed left and right as the sun shined and then clouds passes between and gave shade. There were no flowers of such but between swirled branch nodes their grew buds of sticky gristle that smelled of sweet honey.

Our exploration took us nearer to the mystical plants and we exited to the surface in protective sun shield suits. The closer we walked nearer the mystical plants it was easy to see now that many small hummingbird like creatures swarmed around the plants sucking the nectar of the nodes below circled branches.

Wow Thomas exclaimed. I've never seen any plants that look like these. Their stems grow in spirals while the under nodes produce this sticky resin that these flying small bumblebee-like creatures seem to flourish off of the dripping nectar.

Thomas bagged a sample of the nectar nodes for later study. It smells similar to marijuana but I've never seen any marijuana with such a powerful smell like these plants have. Thankfully I'm protected from any poisonous effects by my suits cloaking ability. Thomas implied.

It can't be too dangerous I said. It doesn't seem to be harmful to the Venus-like hummingbirds. I've captured three of the bee creatures in a Venus airtight container. We'll stow those samples in the cargo bay to analyze with the computers later.

Let's head back to the Rover and be on our way. Okay Thomas said. It want be too long before the sun sets anyway. We've traveled a pretty good distance today. My stomach's growling a bit for some food myself. I could eat a Venus Buffalo just about now.

I grinned as we unsealed the rovers hatch and returned to the safety of Dependence inside. As we traverse on westward towards the setting sun it was decided to travel on as far as possible before the dusk of Venus was upon us. It was such an amazing site to view the rosy Triton Moon hanging just above the setting sun in the forward view screen.

Another hours travel and we parked among the desert shrubby and shut the Dependence Rover down for the night that was approaching by the minute.

Thomas and I had no idea what tomorrows discovery might bring. We decided to engage the rovers high powered telescope shortly after the sun set below the Venus western horizon.

Yesterday Triton was rising an hour or so after sunset. Tonight Triton was lighting Venus with eerie shadows because it was rising 20 minutes after sunset and red rays through the clouds in the Venus dusk were displaying a beautiful cloud spectral sunset.

As stars appeared past sunset I focused the telescope towards the ecliptic and zeroed in on Planet Saturn the most beautiful ringed planet known.

Made mostly of hydrogen helium and methane, Saturn rotates extremely fast on its axis and turns once every 10 hours and 34 minutes.

Saturn rotates so fast that it bulges at the equator by more than ten percent more than it does at the poles.

It takes 29.4 years to revolve around the Sun once and is the farthest planet that can be seen by the naked eye.

In my view finder I easily spotted the Moons Prometheus and Pandora that keeps the F ring together and intact. Saturn has a total of 120 Moons and moonlets in orbit. I could also see Titan, Rhea and Enchiladas as they continued their journey around the beautiful ringed Saturn.

Astronomy had always been my first love from a early age and every time I viewed worlds through a telescope I was always amazed by the wonder of it all. For hours I just sat there viewing the heavens with new wonder. Tomorrows journey awaits as I disengaged the telescope and retired to my quarters to gain the rest that I would surely need for tomorrows further Venus exploration.

CHAPTER 31
First Solar Eclipse on Venus

Today was a special day on Planet Venus. This was the day at 1016 AM on November 12th, that Triton was to perform it's first total solar eclipse of the Sun.

We both awoke at sunrise to hurry along to a specific co-ordinance that the total eclipse could be viewed from that was twenty five kilometers to the west. That would put us in the direct path of Tritons total eclipse of the sun.

We arrived at the specific location at 9 AM Venus time and I became extremely excited of being one of the first to record the first ever total eclipse of the Sun from Venus. Former Earth generations that survived had forgotten the experience and thrill of a solar eclipse.

Earth was no more and the generations that had survived didn't know what to expect when the Moon passed between the Sun and Venus.

The rover with Thomas and I were soon joined by a few more curious first time observers of the not to far away in time phenomenon.

Even though Triton was smaller than the former Earth Moon, it was placed closer to Venus than Earth's Moon and due to its smaller size, it would almost completely cover the Sun at totality.

At 10:16 AM, wonder and awe filled the eyes of the observers as Triton appeared to touch the edge the Sun corona.

As the minutes passed all were excited as the Suns brightness began to dim as Triton now half covered the bright star.

Several more minutes passed and darkness fell upon Venus as totality occurred. There was an eerie darkness that fell upon the land. Rosy shimmering shadows projected through Tritons atmosphere displaying mysterious darkness all around the area.

Spectators were in awe as baily's beads occurred on the edge of the solar disk. It only lasted 30 seconds and after another minute passed the Sun began revealing its glory behind the Triton Moon.

It was indeed a fantastic site from Venus that the new inhabitants of this world had never experienced before.

Eerie calmness prevailed and not a sound was heard from the small crowd until Triton had again revealed the total sunshine by the solar systems faithful star the Sun.

By 10:31 AM, the fantastic stellar show was over and Venusians began returning to their chariot vehicles to begin departing the area.

After all is said and done, we didn't call ourselves Earthlings anymore.

Yes, we were still human beings but we were now considered to be Venusians.

By 11:00 AM, Thomas and I had stowed away our telescopic recorder and had also departed the area headed towards one more exploration goal approximately 70 kilometers to the north of our present eclipse viewing location.

At 10 mph, the 44 miles took about four and a half hours to arrive at our finale destination before after one more night on Venus we would have to return to Pandora city tomorrow.

The rovers resources and power supply had dwindled to 40 % by the time we reached our new destination around 5;30 PM Venus time. All along the journey the thump of the tree planter was heard as we progressed onward towards another destination.

We drove three kilometers further along a streams winding boundary until we approached a level clearing lake surrounded by many colored flowered vegetations. Such a lovely site I reported to Thomas. This looks like a good place to spend the night before we have return to Pandora tomorrow.

This time we were following a flowing river stream that ran east and west among a narrow band of low mountain hilly terrene and this stream fed the lake that we were approaching and going to camp next to for the night.

Nearly 6 PM Venus time, Thomas and I decided to sample the lake and see what sort of fish had been transported to Venus from the former planet Earth.

The temperature outside just before dusk had cooled to 80 degrees Fahrenheit as we both cast our lines into the beautiful Venus lake.

A hour passed and I had caught three two pound fish and Thomas had reeled in two also.

I commented to Thomas, You know a fish that weighed a pound on the former earth would only weigh a little over eighty percent of a pound on Venus. Thomas laughed and said that may be true but these two pound fish that we caught on Venus would weigh over two and a half pounds had we caught them on Earth.

It seemed such a perfect end to the Venus exploration journey when suddenly the Rover's alarm sounded and Thomas and I rushed to the rover to comprehend the situation.

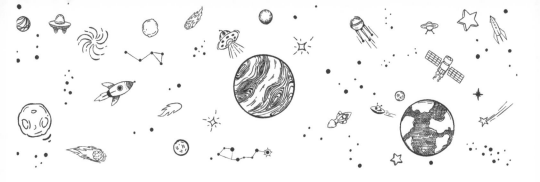

CHAPTER 32
Buried Under Venus Mud

Suddenly the atmosphere produced a deep rumble and a 10 meter fireball glowed hotter as it approached the lake. It's over 30 feet in diameter Thomas said excitedly. We'd better engage the force field. Just as I flipped the switch the meteor crashed into the center of the lake with a loud whoosh and for a fraction of a second, silence filled the cabin as all the water in the lake propelled upward and came crashing back down on the entire surrounding area.

The force field did its job in protecting the rover but now it was trapped in a huge mudslide that was rushing back towards the rover and crew.

Thomas quickly began spinning the tracks to meet the mud slide head on but the rovers force field was not capable of withstanding total protection of the amount of mud water that the rover was crashing into.

The force field was still working but now they were trapped beneath an air bubble covered with the Venus mud slide that the meteor had caused when it crashed into the lake.

There we sat covered in mud with no hope of sending a rescue signal that could reach any concerned soul. We were doubtful that even radar could detect the rover under meters of mud.

Emergency lighting suddenly engaged inside the under mud dark rover and Thomas and I were for the first time in our exploration extremely concerned.

What can we do now Thomas exclaimed nervously. The rover can't move inside the protective shield with the weight of all of that mud that's on top of it.

Even so I stated. We're broadcasting an emergency signal anyway. It's always possible someone will hear the signal and rescue us.

Above the rover was nighttime on Venus and long hours dragged by as the crew anticipated some sort of a response from their emergency signal. Due to the excess mud coverage of the rover, by assumed sunrise the air supply had dwindled to 15 percent remaining and that included the air inside the protective bubble of the force field.

We were indeed very trapped but I Celesta was not about to concede to being buried alive on Venus.

I immediately began searching the computer to explore a possible solution to our dire straight situation. Hours of searching the computer database finally offered the only possible solution that could possibly help Thomas and I survive.

Here it is I said.

This rover archive article says it is possible to point the remaining forcefield in a forward direction and spin the force field up in a clockwise direction acting as a drill bit in front of the rovers path.

It also states that the forward movement will be slow but it's the only chance that we have to get out of this muddy mess. It also says that if our remaining power supply dwindles below 10 percent, that the force field will cease to exist. We're at 38% power remaining in the rovers batteries now. We need to hurry up and give this solution a try.

Agreed Thomas said as he began to input rovers computer with the proper sequence of codes to begin the process.

The rover shook as Thomas engaged the order to begin the process of clockwise spinning the forcefield ahead of the under the mud rover. Immediately the power supply dropped to 35 % as the strain of the rotating forcefield engaged and the rover inched 15 degrees upward in a inch by inch progression.

It may take hours for us to break out Thomas said but it is our only hope of survival. With the force field's spinning motion our air supply has already dropped to 10 percent remaining. We definitely need to stay calm and breathe slowly to conserve air.

Agreed I said. As I sat back in my seat and shut my eyes expressing to myself a prayer to the Almighty Creator to please let us survive.

It seemed as the hours of slow forward motion were passing, I kept continuously opening my eyes to view the rover's power supply remaining. The power was now down to 13 % and the radar through the mud was not capable of penetrating to the surface. I also knew that if the rovers power supply reached below 10 percent that the spinning force field would cease to drill and collapse around the rover.

Once more I closed my eyes after I observed a nervous sweat developing upon Thomas's forehead as he kept pushing forward on the joy stick control.

The last thing I remember was seeing 11 percent on the power supply meter and the thinning air had began to make me extremely woozy. Then I remember the sound of nothingness as the rovers motors shut down and silence and darkness filled the cabin.

The air was very thin inside and I had trouble breathing but I could barely see a tiny glint of light at the nose of the rover's forward tip. With all my remaining strength, I looked over to see Thomas unconscious in the drivers seat. I knew that the rover has a forward escape hatch that was concealed under the control panel and I somehow managed to crawl upward to the point of the release that immediately allowed fresh air to fill the rover.

Thomas was awakened from the blast of fresh air and immediately began to follow me as I pushed the remaining mud away so that we both could crawl out exhausted to the welcome Venus surface above the rovers nose.

Thank God our prayers had been answered and we had survived. I can't remember how long we both lay there on top of the mud before we gained enough strength but it was quite a while before we stood up and viewed the scene around us.

As we finally stood and surveyed the scene. The rovers hatch lay open just below the top of the mud level and in the direction of the former full lake that was now only half as large as it once was, the lake was surrounded by a large downward sloped smooth mud ring that we had just barely survived below the meteors mud wrath.

After a bit of exhausted rest Thomas reentered the front of the rovers hatch that was slightly sticking out of the mud. He came back out with a cable and electric wench and managed to attach the long end of the cable to a large boulder 30 feet in front of the rover and the other end to the winch that he attached to the eye hook on the tip of the rover's exposed surface.

We both hoped the rover had enough remaining power to pull itself free from the mud pit that it was mired up in. If we could pull the rover from the mud, then it would be possible to attach a solar recharger in order to charge the rover's batteries in order to return us back safely to Pandora base.

The rover winch slowed and strained its last electric power just enough to pull itself free. The solar power hook up was easy but Thomas and I had to spend several hours cleaning the mud from the rover tracks so that they could turn once the rover was recharged enough to head towards home.

Once the rover had gained enough power, we were able to contact home base to inform them of our situation and let them know that we were alright and would be returning after the rovers batteries were recharged.

Thomas and I spent the rest of the Venus daylight cleaning ourselves up and checking out the rovers total status. All appeared well and the batteries were at a 60% recharge state by the time the Sun was setting in the western Venus sky. We both watched the amazing colored sunset.

We soon retired to spend another night in the rover to analyze the situation and ready ourselves for tomorrows journey back to Pandora base.

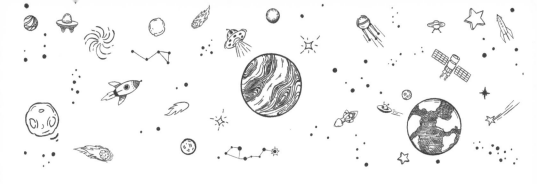

CHAPTER 33

Return to Pandora Base

November 14th, 3915, 615 AM

After an early morning snack, Thomas and I engaged the solar recharger to soak up the early morning Venus rays. By 10 Am we had attached the solar panel to the top of the rover and were all set to return to base.

We were almost 120 kilometers or 75 miles away from home and I now piloted the rover in the direction that would get us home. If all went well, we should be at the base in seven and a half hours.

We traversed the hills and flatlands around craters and streams in a steady journey for six hours. Suddenly, when we were several miles from base, unexpectedly the right side's track broke into and we were at a stand still and unable to drive the rover further towards Pandora base.

The track had broken and ripped away from its sprocket and we didn't have a spare track to install. We were able to radio home base and a rescue copter was soon on the way with spare parts

5:30 PM the parts arrived and in a hours time Thomas had the rover operational again.

One important lesson that we learned is that it just wasn't safe to take off exploring New Venus without another rover party of explorers along.

As we rolled into Pandora base, the Sun was setting ahead of another Venus storm on that thankful day of November 14th, 3915.

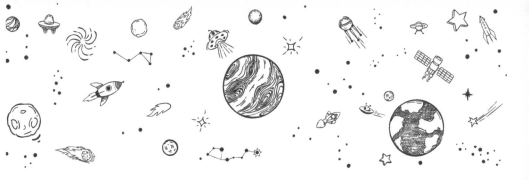

CHAPTER 34
Our Report to
The Exploration Council

November 15th, 3915 10:00 AM

Thomas and I stood before the Venus Exploration Council that morning to report our exploration journals to the head Council of seven members.

The facts above were as recorded and our finale conclusion and opinion was, that Venus was still dangerous but next time exploration should be required to be four member in two separate rovers in order to be more safe.

The Head Exploration Council thanked Thomas and I and we left them with the hard drive that contained our exploration chronicles and all that had happened to us on our four days journey to places on Venus that had never been explored before.

Venus in the year 3916

I Celesta had began recording our journey for my own personal files, I realized that no matter what I thought of the days before Earth's destruction, It was now my home Planet Venus that all humans that had survived will have a future here.

This planet from now on will forever be considered to be our home world.

Venus still had a ways to go to match the beauty and safety of the former Earth. But in due time, We future Venusians will continue to work hard at the Revival of Venus. We surely could and would make it so.

Venus' future was in ours and the Creators hand's best interests.

With an extreme struggle to survive, Venus was now the home world of all of us surviving Venusians.

Venus' population in 3916 was just over one billion souls. The New Triton Moon was doing its job in regulating the tilt on Venus' axis and creating tides and seasons. The revived oceans on Venus were still being bombarded with ice meteors from the asteroid belt by Repulse Attracter ships on a regular basis.

The atmosphere had settled to 98% of the former Earth's properties and temperatures near the equator had dropped to 110 degrees Fahrenheit.

Temperatures were considerably cooler as you traveled north or south of the equator. Snowy white ice caps had developed at both poles and ice meteors were being injected there also.

It had taken several centuries to make this new world Venus habitable for humans to survive. We were indeed open to enable humankind's future possibilities.

We did what we had to do to insure this future that we were to have from this day forward.

We surviving Venusians are proof that under extreme circumstances, We can accomplish miracles. We did just that. No it wasn't easy at all. The Almighty and our technology of the day, was what helped us win this battle.

If you are in Venus' future and are somehow reading these Venus Chronicles, Your rapture will never be coming with a collision with the Nibiru. The Nibiru planet that had plagued our solar system for eons was now gone forever also.

The Almighty Creator used Earth to destroy this evil rogue world.

I Celesta Marcia, do morn for the lost souls but I am indeed grateful for the survival of the billion that survived the Nibiru here on the new world Planet Venus.

Thanks to the Creator of all, Venus is safe for now. Let's all hope that humankind doesn't mess this world up like humans had done to Planet Earth.

Perhaps its time to journey outward from this solar system. The Milky Way Galaxy has many places to visit and explore. Looking through a telescope is fine. But it takes courage and determination to venture to the stars.

I'm willing to bet my last Venusian's bar of Galena Gold, that in a thousand more Venus years, human-kind will travel to the stars and discover amazing new worlds. But for now, Venus has provided us all a new hope that one day, Our survival at Venus will make that happen.

We are indeed grateful to the Creators Messengers the Anunnaki that helped humankind survive the Nibiru's passing many times over the eons of humankinds past.

We sincerely hoped that they also survived their worlds destruction. Possibly one day in the future, we'll meet up again to thank them personally for caring enough to warn us of Earth's destruction.

If You can imagine the possibilities, you are more than half way home.

CHAPTER 35

Heroes by Eric Wilkins

As a final poetry of words, I offer this poem devoted to the twentieth century astronauts that gave their all and perished in the Columbia and Challenger disasters.

Heroes by Eric Wilkins
In Honor of the Columbia and Challenger Astronauts

Condolence intended silence in place
Mission extended with tears upon face
Heroes remembered bravest of best
Columbia and Challenger in heaven now rest
Universal dimensions of galaxies unknown
Potential unlimited there where you roam
A place of serenity past twinkling of stars
Knowledge of journeys beginning past mars
Generations of future stand to the call
Seekers of knowledge givers of all
Salute to the heroes explorers delight
The bravest of heroes sail high upon flight
The wind is your vector much courage indeed
Honors of valor your mission succeeds
The sun in its setting the moons crescent tear
Remind us of all the heroes honored here
The wispier of clouds the blueness below
The path that you lead for others to go
Will lead to the stars because heroes like you
Gave of their all the things heroes do.

Copyright ©2005 Eric Wilkins

ABOUT THE AUTHOR

Full Name, Donald Eric Wilkins. But! I have always gone by Eric Wilkins my entire life and I always will.

Born, 1157 pm December 24, 1950

Henderson N. C.

Loved Astronomy from early age.

Lived many years on this Fantastic Spaceship Earth.

My Bucket List is almost full and I will soon go on to explore the Universe.

The Earth is moving toward Leo at the dizzying speed of 390 kilometers a second. That's a little over 242 miles per second.

You're on it too. God speed!